T0055862

SUPERNATURAL

KAZ 215

Mini Guide to Saving People and Hunting Things

INSIGHT EDITIONS

San Rafael, California

THE WINCHESTERS

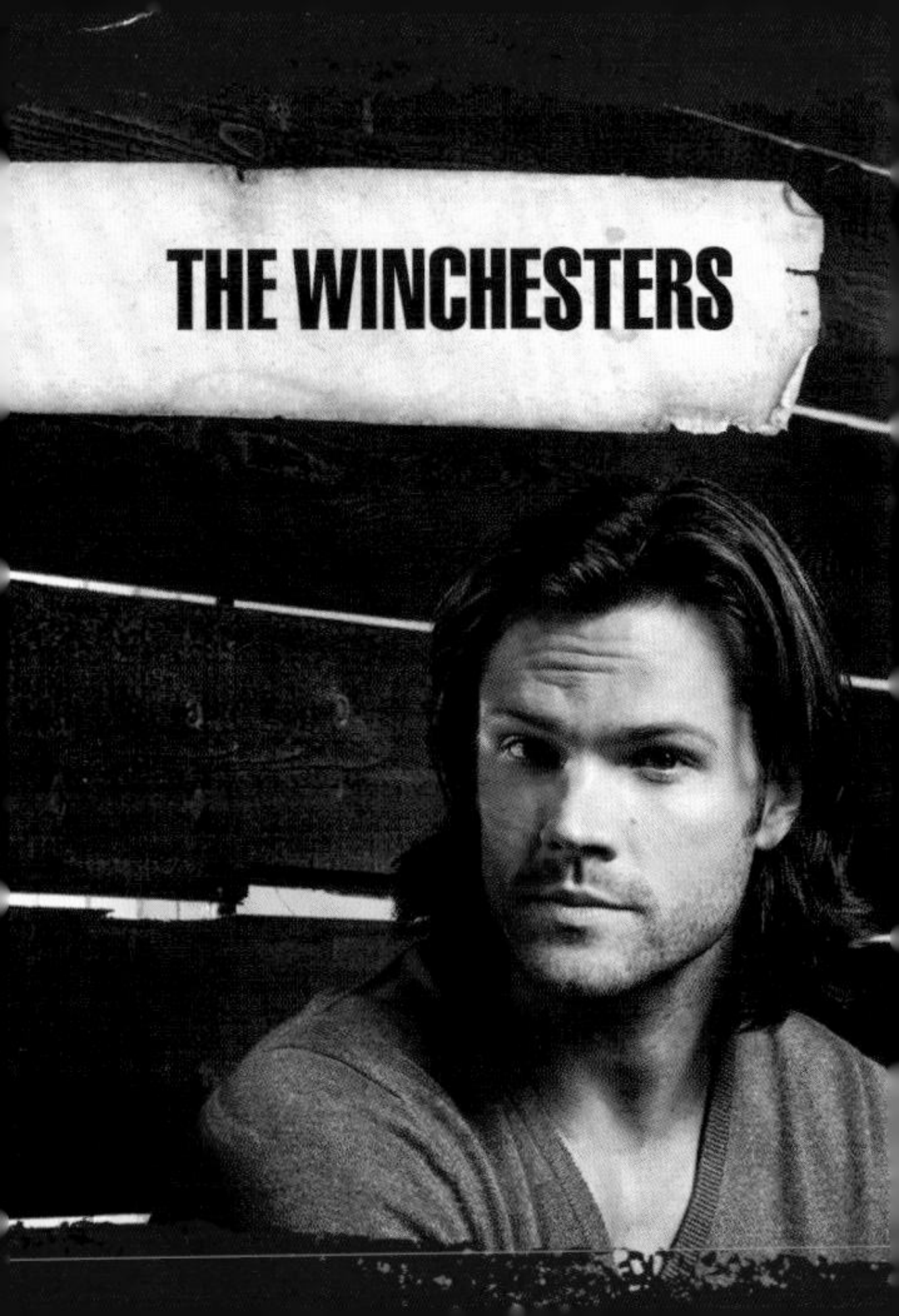

SAM WINCHESTER

On November 2, 1983, a baby named Sam Winchester was visited by a yellow-eyed demon that dripped its blood into the infant's mouth. Sam's mother, Mary, tried to stop the demon but was killed. This traumatic event set the Winchester family on the path to becoming a clan of unstoppable monster hunters.

DEAN WINCHESTER

Dean Winchester is the elder Winchester brother. After Mary's death, John Winchester took his sons on the road across the United States on his quest for revenge. Hunting Azazel, the Yellow-Eyed Demon, and killing other evil creatures the family encounters along the way is the perfect life for Dean: He's a good son and a good soldier.

"I've been following you around my entire life. I mean, I've been looking up to you since I was four, Dean. Studying you, trying to be just like my big brother. So yeah, I know you. Better than anyone else in the entire world."

—SAM WINCHESTER

"Once a wise man told me, 'Family don't end in blood.' But it doesn't start there either. Family cares about you. Not what you can do for them. Family is there for the good, bad, all of it. They got your back. Even when it hurts. That's family."

—DEAN WINCHESTER

JOHN WINCHESTER

John Winchester married the love of his life, Mary Campbell, and they had two sons, Dean and Sam. But that's where the fairy tale ended and the nightmare began, with Mary's murder by Azazel in Sam's nursery. Seeking vengeance, John devotes his life to hunting the demon.

MARY WINCHESTER

Mary Winchester, née Campbell, lived a life of adventure before she met John. Her parents, Samuel and Deanna Campbell, were hunters, as was most of her family before her, stretching back generations. Mary kept her past secret from John for fear of losing him or worse. Unfortunately, her fears were warranted.

ADAM, THE UNKNOWN WINCHESTER

Adam Milligan is the son of Kate Milligan and John Winchester, though he didn't meet his father until he was twelve and only found out about the existence of supernatural monsters when he was killed by a ghoul. Adam later became the archangel Michael's vessel and is now trapped with Lucifer and Michael in Lucifer's cage in Hell.

HENRY WINCHESTER

Henry was John Winchester's father and therefore Dean and Sam's grandfather. He first met his grandchildren when he was sent to the year 2013 after fleeing the demon Abaddon back in 1958. Henry, like his father before him, was one of the Men of Letters, a group of learned people who study, research, and combat all things supernatural.

"I didn't know my son as a man, but having met you two, I know I would have been proud of him."

—HENRY WINCHESTER

KA

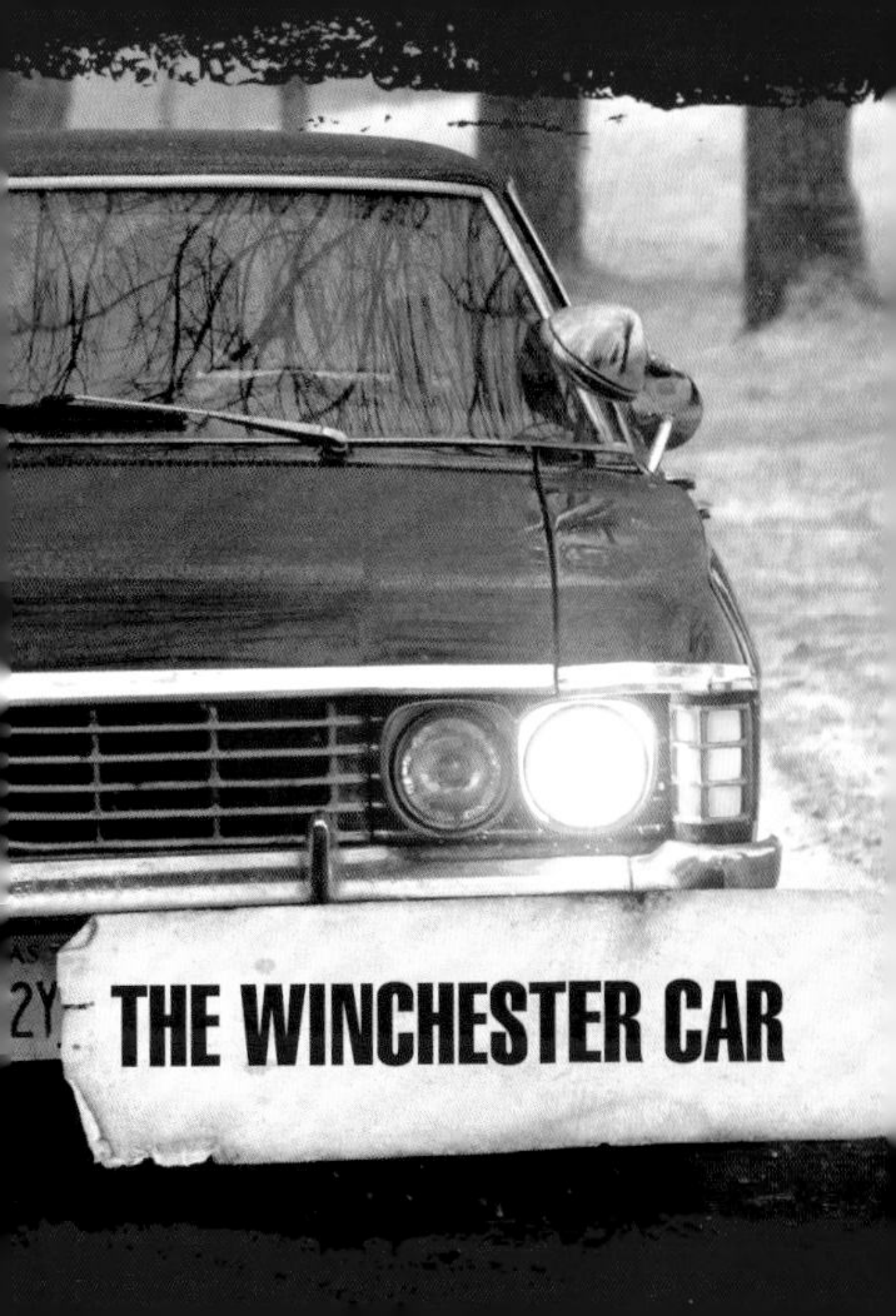
2Y
THE WINCHESTER CAR

The Winchesters' car is an automatic, four-door hardtop with a black exterior that does double duty as stylish transportation and sleeping quarters for Sam and Dean. Passed down to Dean by his father, the sleek black car has been lovingly customized by both Winchesters over the years.

The car is perfect for hunting as the trunk can hold a massive weapons arsenal, two duffel bags of clothes, and a body (human or monster). More important, it has a cassette player radio—iPod jacks are not welcome.

"Driver picks the music;
shotgun shuts his cakehole."
—DEAN WINCHESTER

THE WEAPONS CACHE

There are countless things hidden in the weapons cache found in the car's trunk, but a few items can be found in the car almost all of the time, including Sam and Dean's favorite handguns, a flare gun used to kill a wendigo the brothers encountered, the stake used to "kill" the Trickster, and a knife passed down to Dean from John Winchester.

2Y5

AFTERMARKET ACCESSORIES

Rosary
Knives
Assorted blades
Wooden stakes
Hex bags
Shotguns
Rifles
Pistols
Axe
Holy water
Dream catcher

A HUNTER'S TOOLS

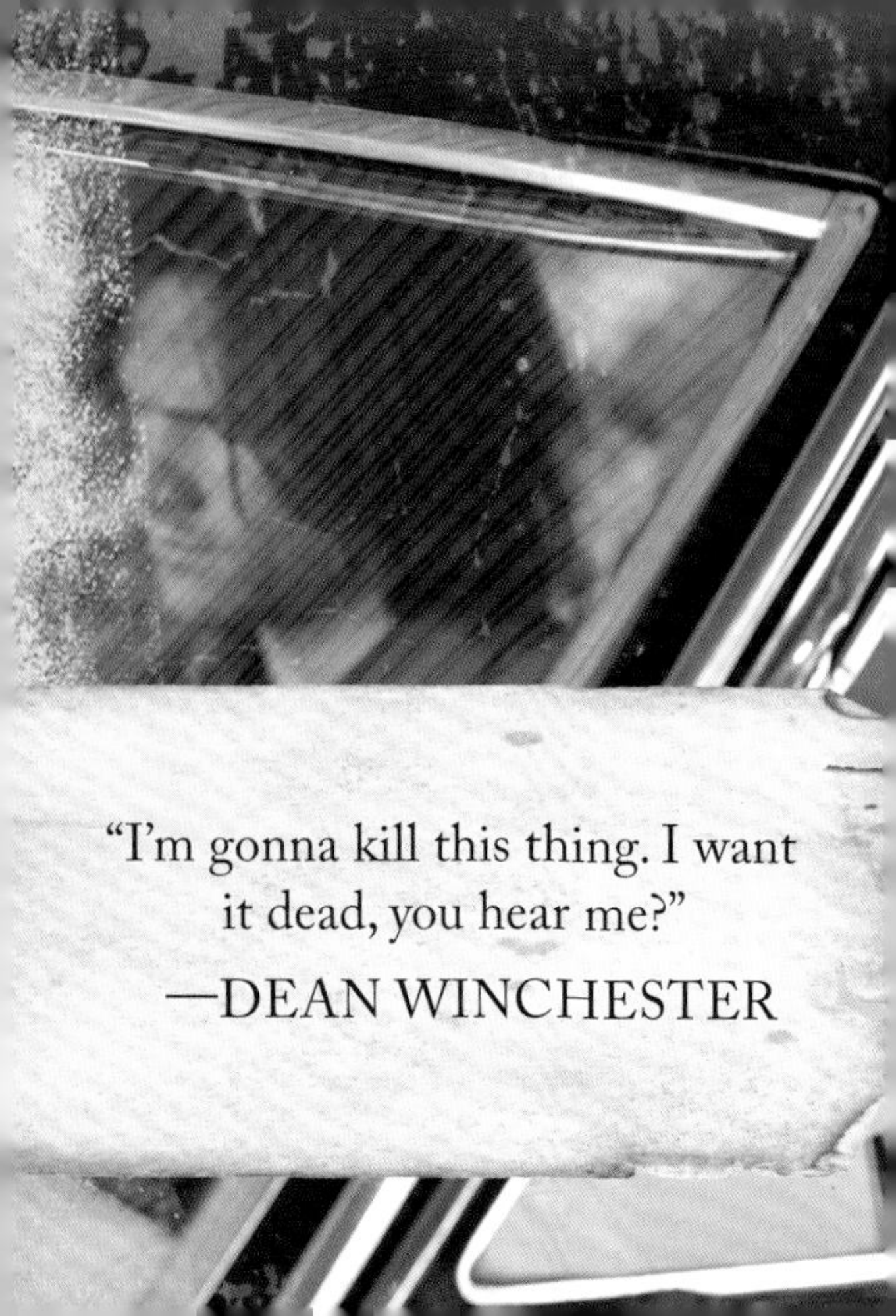

"I'm gonna kill this thing. I want it dead, you hear me?"

—DEAN WINCHESTER

AXE

An essential weapon for a hunter, as it can be used to decapitate monsters (such as vampires and Leviathan—creatures created by God and imprisoned due to their unstable nature).

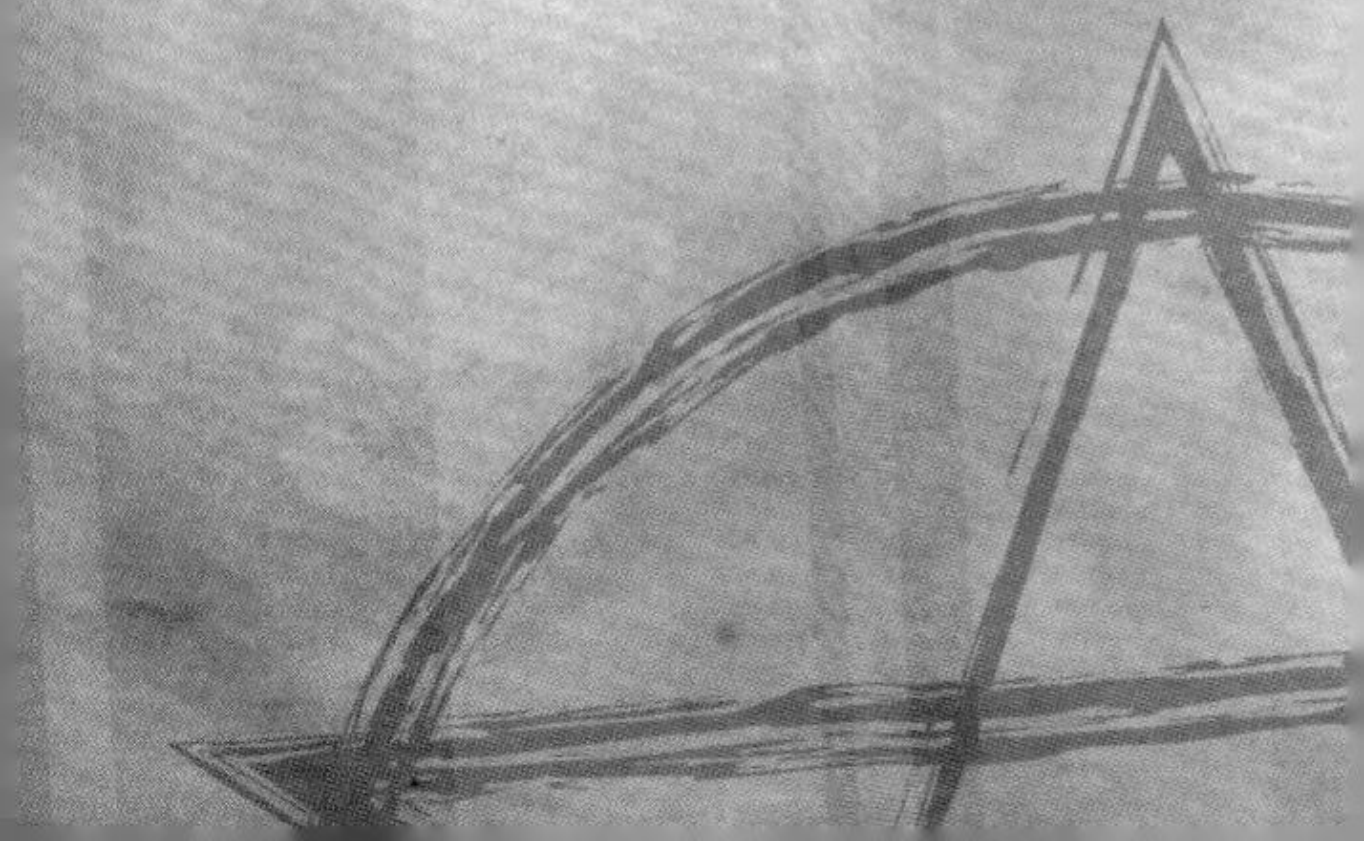

BAMBOO DAGGER

Kills ōkami (fanged Japanese monsters who feed on humans) if it's properly blessed by a Shinto priest, but the monster must be stabbed exactly seven times, or it is not truly dead.

BLOOD

Dead humans' blood poisons vampires; dog's blood poisons some pagan gods (such as Veritas, the Goddess of Truth); dragon's blood is needed to kill dragons; lamb's blood is needed to kill djinn. Blood is also an essential ingredient in most summoning and banishment spells.

BRASS

Blades, steam organ pipes, etc.

Kills rakshasa (shapeshifting demons who feed on human flesh); it also has repelling properties.

BRONZE BLADE

Kills sirens, primarily, but it is also a convenient weapon when dealing with "regular" monsters.

CAMERA

A camera's flash will briefly immobilize creatures that are used to the dark; the viewfinder reveals ghosts and the flare in shapeshifters' or other types of monsters' eyes.

CHAIN SAW

Decapitates most monsters and will momentarily incapacitate just about any creature until it can be killed.

CREAM

Inebriates faeries, according to ancient lore and firsthand experience by Dean and Sam Winchester.

CROSSBOW

Depends on the supernatural strength of the monsters, but regular projectile usage applies.

CURSE BOXES

Keeps cursed objects from affecting those who handle the boxes. Essential when dealing with magical items but must be locked properly.

DEVIL'S TRAP

A Devil's Trap is a supernatural sigil used to trap demons and bind them in place. It can be drawn with anything from paint to flaming blueberry vodka. However, the instant the sigil's lines are broken in the slightest, the demon can escape. Devil's Traps can also be handy as deterrents to keep demons out of places like car trunks, storage lockers, and panic rooms.

ELECTRO MAGNETIC
LOW
DANGER
18

ELECTROMAGNETIC FIELD (EMF) METER

Locates ghosts and is perhaps one of the most essential tools a hunter can have in their arsenal. Most are homemade.

FIRE

Blowtorches, disposable lighters, flare guns, matches, etc.

Kills changelings, crocotta (creatures that take human form to feed on humans' souls), ghouls, rugaru (flesh-eating monsters), and wendigos. Fire is a natural tool for hunters, given that most creatures are susceptible to it.

GUN

Handguns, shotguns, sniper rifles, etc.

Slows down just about any monster and, with the proper ammo, can also kill them. Regular bullets can kill Amazons, witches, ghouls, and zombies.

HEX BAG

Hides the bearer from demons. Can also be used to wreak havoc if hidden in a person's home, vehicle, or clothing.

HOLY WATER

Harms and repels demons. Can be used by direct application or by wetting weapons with the blessed liquid.

IRIDIUM

Axes, bullets, knives, swords, etc.

Kills alpha monsters. As alpha monsters are rare and hard to kill, it is essential that your iridium-forged weapon is clean and sharp.

IRON

Axes, buckshot, bullets, chains, knives, nails, etc.

Dispels ghosts; keeps demons, faeries, and phoenixes (creatures who turn their victims to ash) at bay or traps them; and kills shtrigas and some pagan gods (such as leshii).

KNIFE

Depends on the supernatural strength of the monster, but regular blade usage applies. A standard weapon for every hunter's arsenal.

LOCKPICKS

Their use is self-explanatory, but they are essential tools of the trade for hunters, so it is important to keep quite a few in various shapes and sizes handy.

MACHETE

Ideal for decapitating monsters such as arachne, as well as vampires and Leviathan.

MIRROR

Shows the true faces of changelings, sirens, and wraiths, and is a useful tool to quickly reveal the true nature of anybody you suspect to be a monster in disguise.

PALO SANTO

Holy wood that is toxic to demons and serves the same purpose as holy water in repelling or harming—but not killing—these creatures of Satan.

RAM'S HORN

Kills some pagan gods (such as Osiris) and can often be found in synagogues.

SALT

Circles of salt and salt lines across entryways can keep out ghosts and demons. Shotgun blasts of rock salt dispel ghosts.

SILVER

Axes, bullets, knives, stakes, swords, etc.

Kills djinn, shapeshifters, skinwalkers, vetalas (creatures that sedate their victims with a toxin and feed on them for days), wendigos, werewolves, wraiths, and zombies. Having silver on hand when facing most monsters and creatures is essential.

SUGAR

When sugar is spilled in front of faeries, they have to stop what they're doing and count every grain.

SWORD

Perfect for decapitating monsters (such as Leviathan); kills dragons (when coated in dragons' blood); and kills shōjō (when consecrated by a Shinto blessing).

TASER

Electrocutes rawheads but is also handy for incapacitating a variety of monsters or even belligerent humans.

WOODEN STAKE

Made out of Babylonian cypress, evergreen, etc. Kills pagan gods, the Whore of Babylon, and tricksters.

SPECIAL WEA

THE COLT

In 1835, Samuel Colt assembled a very special gun. While its barrel is the key that unlocks the Devil's Gate he built in Wyoming, he ultimately built the weapon for hunting supernatural creatures. It has a pentagram on the handle and is engraved with Latin words that translate to *I will fear no evil.*

Legend says this gun can kill anything, although that's not quite true. It kills demons, vampires, and phoenixes without a problem, but it can't kill Lucifer. The fallen archangel claims there are four other things in all of creation it can't kill—likely the other three archangels, and Death.

Samuel Colt made thirteen numbered silver bullets for the gun, of which five remained when John Winchester came into

possession of the weapon, and, with John and his sons making full use of it, the bullets soon ran out.

THE DEMON-KILLING KNIFE

Ruby appeared with her special knife that could kill demons—and only demons—as readily as the Colt.

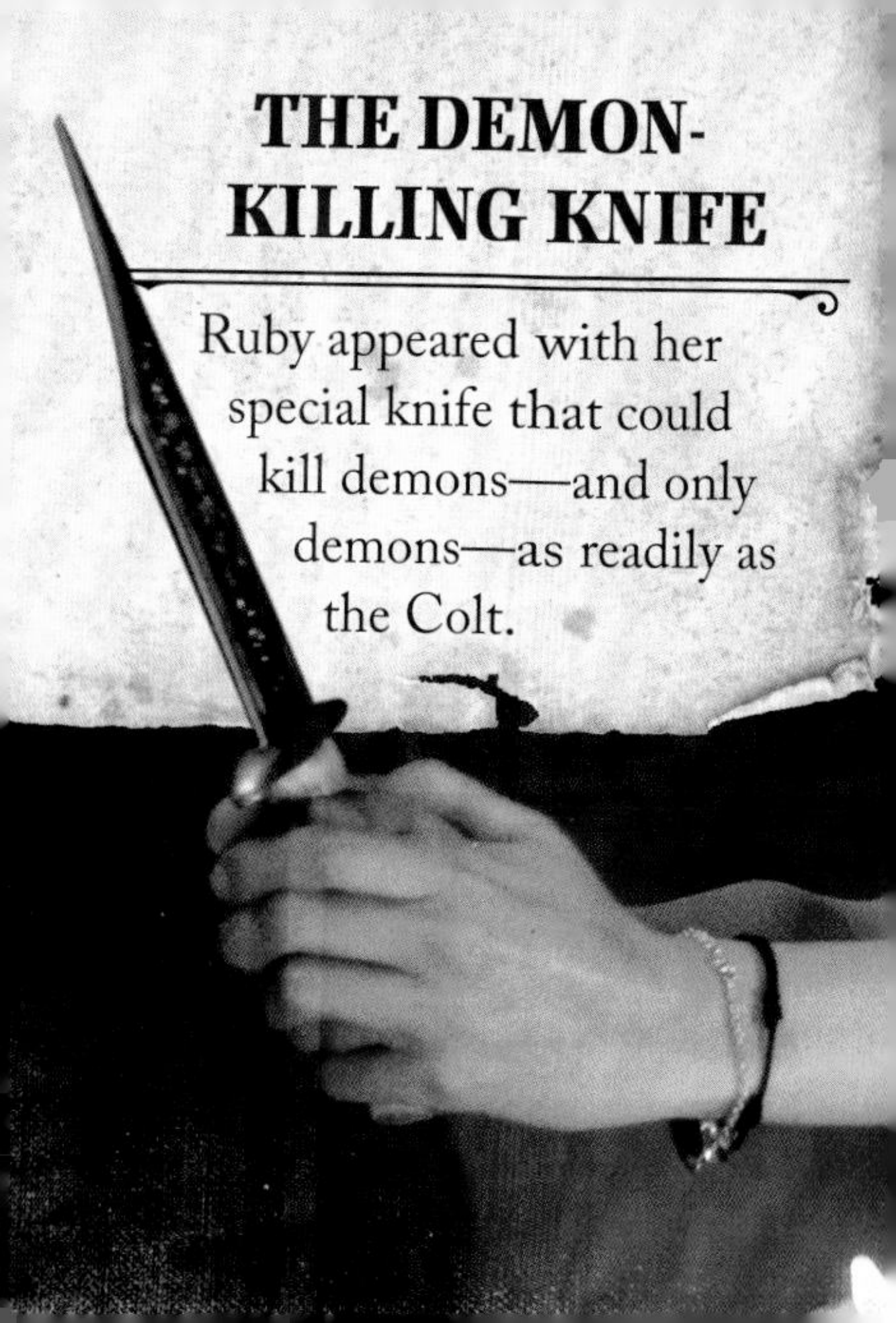

The demon-killing knife's origins are unknown, and the engravings on its blade are unknowable, but it seems likely Ruby made it

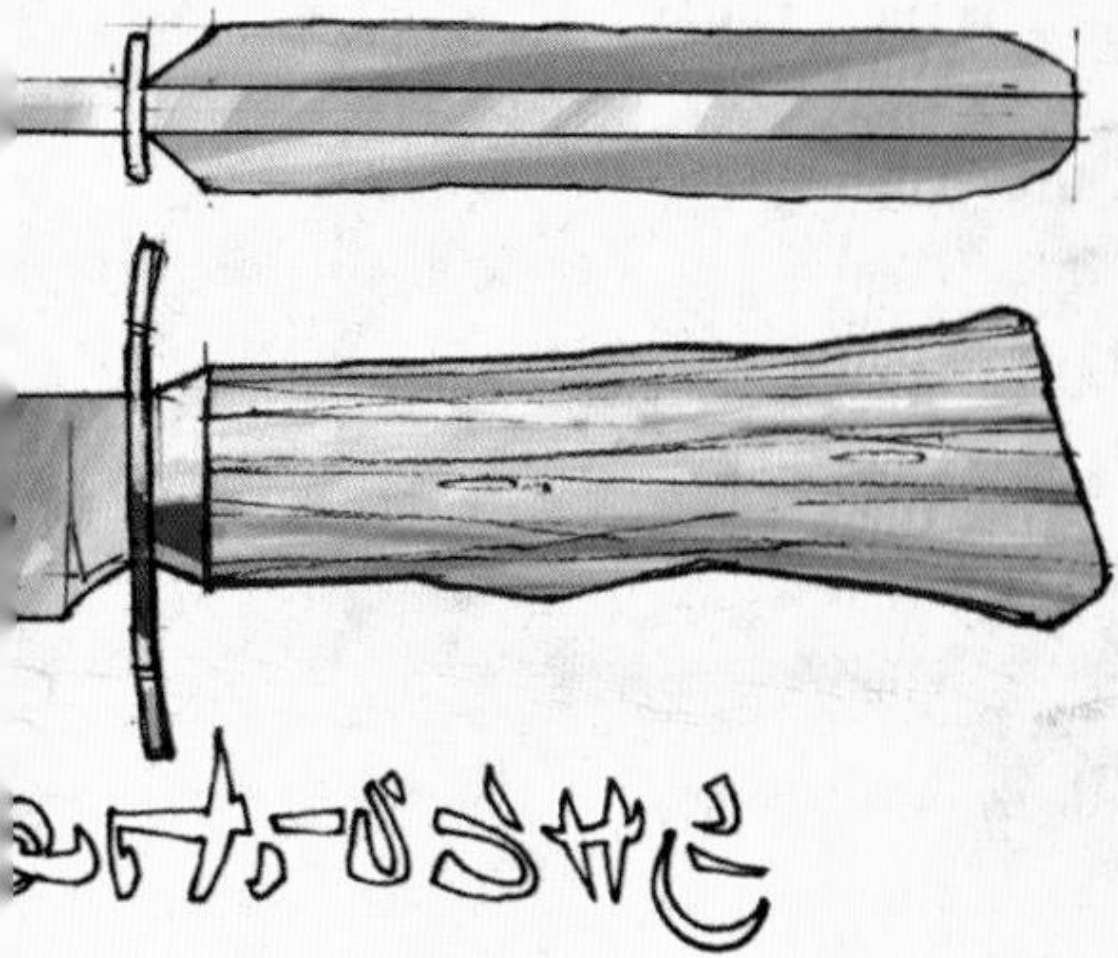

herself since she had the know-how to make the Colt work again without Samuel's magic bullets, a skill she shared with Bobby Singer.

THE FIRST BLADE

Cain, the leader of the Knights of Hell, forged the First Blade from the donkey's jawbone he used to kill his brother, Abel. It is the only known weapon that can kill Abaddon. Cain's mark is the source of the First Blade's power, and he can only transfer it to someone worthy to bear it. Despite the dangers, Dean agrees to wear the mark so that he can wield the blade.

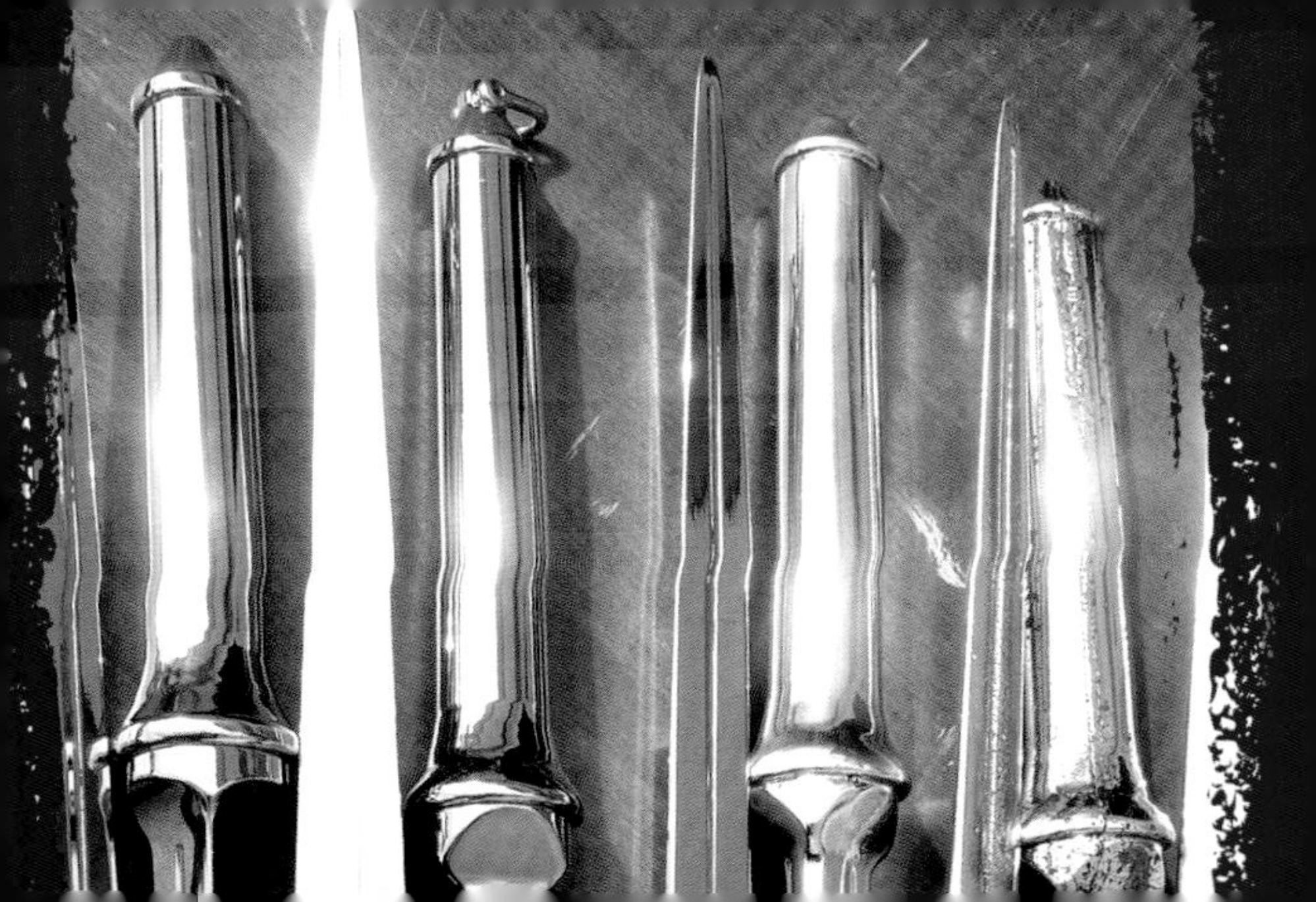

HEAVENLY WEAPONS

ANGEL BLADE

Aka the angel-killing dagger. It's unknown what alloy this weapon is made of, and it's unlikely that its original purpose was to kill angels, but during the war in Heaven, that becomes its primary use.

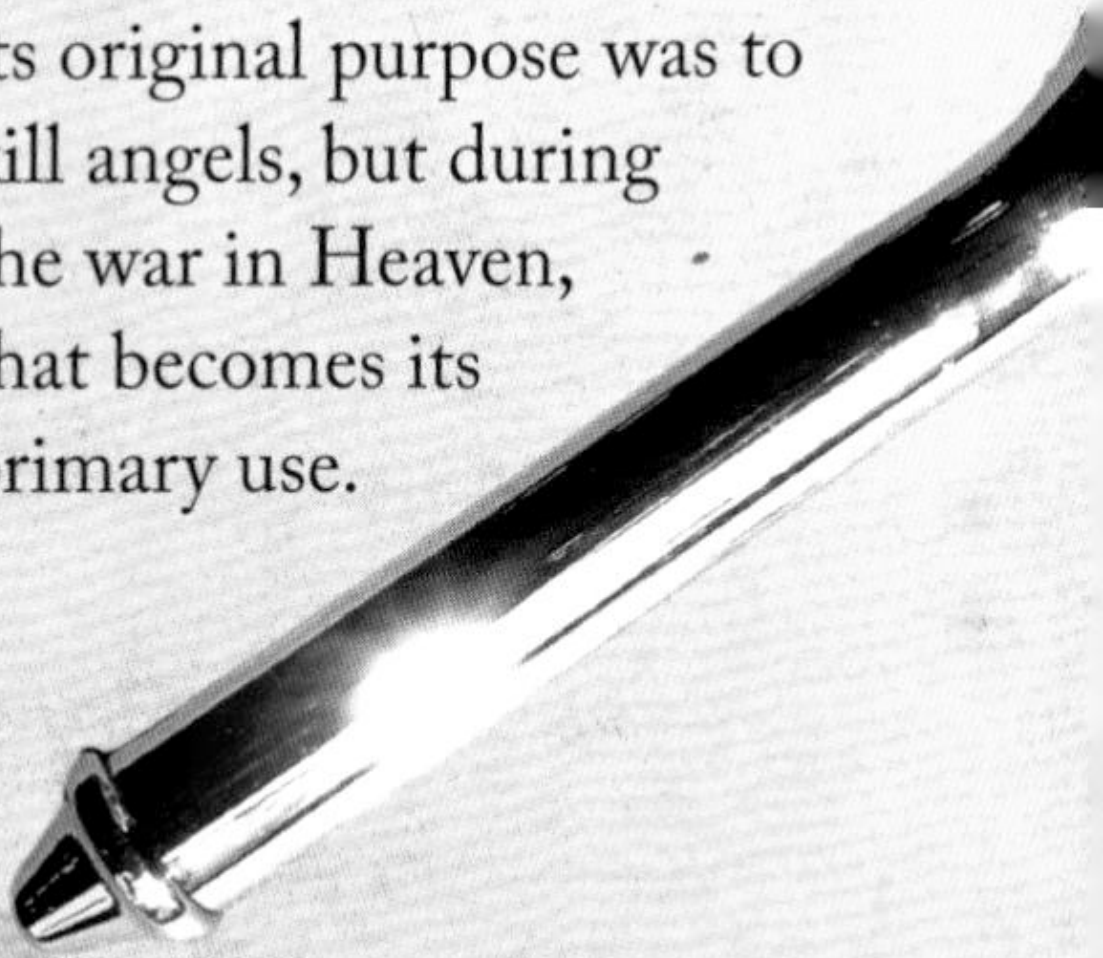

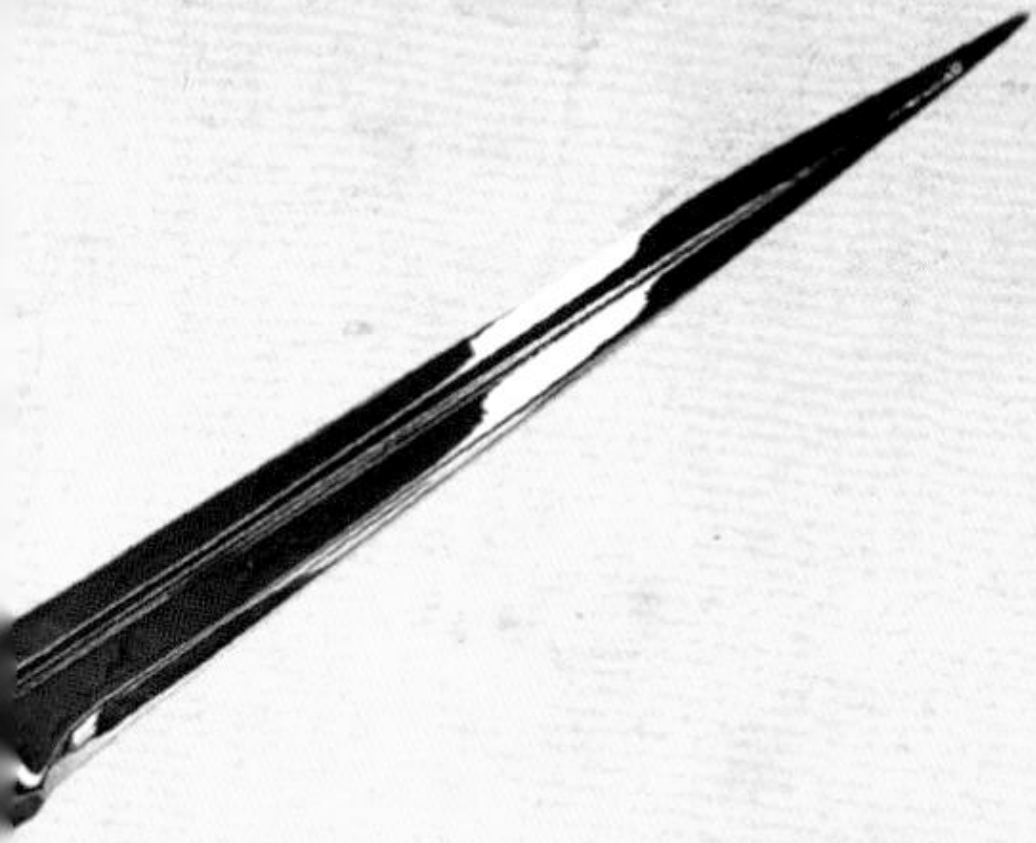

However, the blade is equally efficient at killing Hellhounds—and, no doubt, humans, too. Heavenly power is imbued in the blade, allowing it to be used effectively by anyone, including demons and humans.

ARCHANGEL BLADE

Looks the same as an angel blade to mortal eyes, but it's been supercharged (presumably from being wielded by an archangel) and is capable of killing even the most powerful of angels.

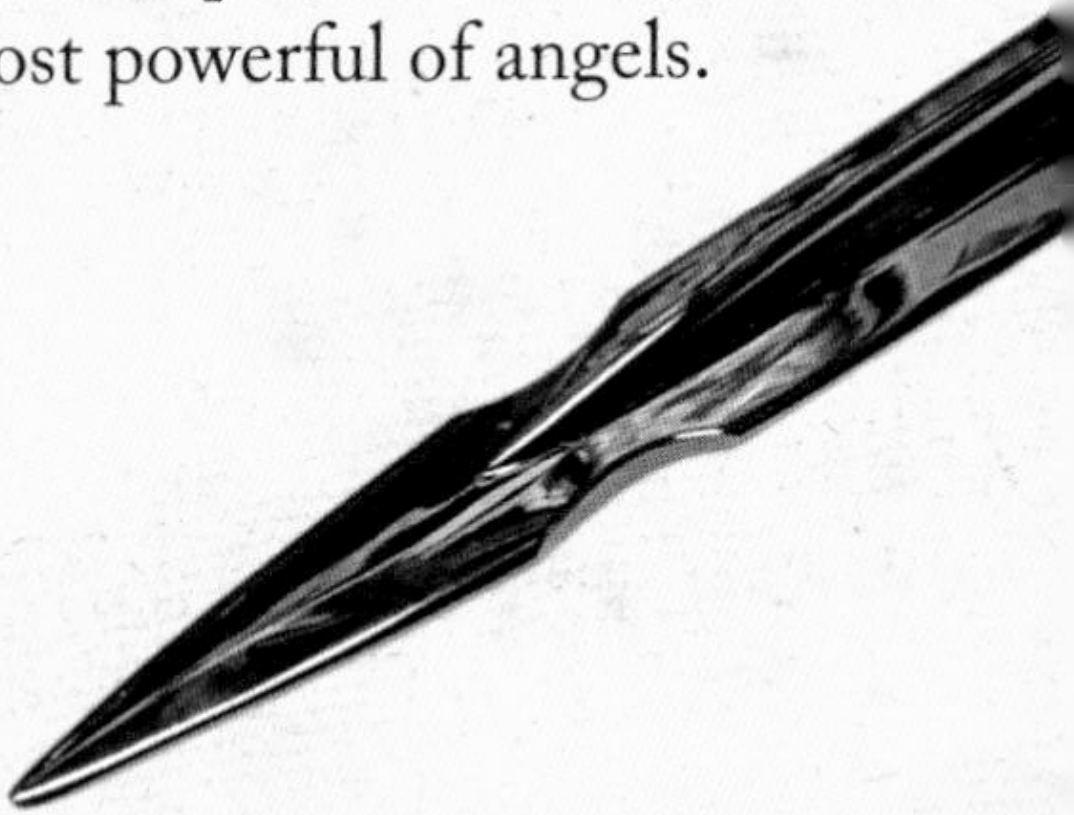

HEAVENLY BLADE

A rare modification of the angel blade, which has been fine-tuned to kill powerful gods like the Fates.

STAFF OF MOSES

The staff can control water, cover people in boils, and summon a plague of locusts, among other things. The staff can also transform into a snake and is effective

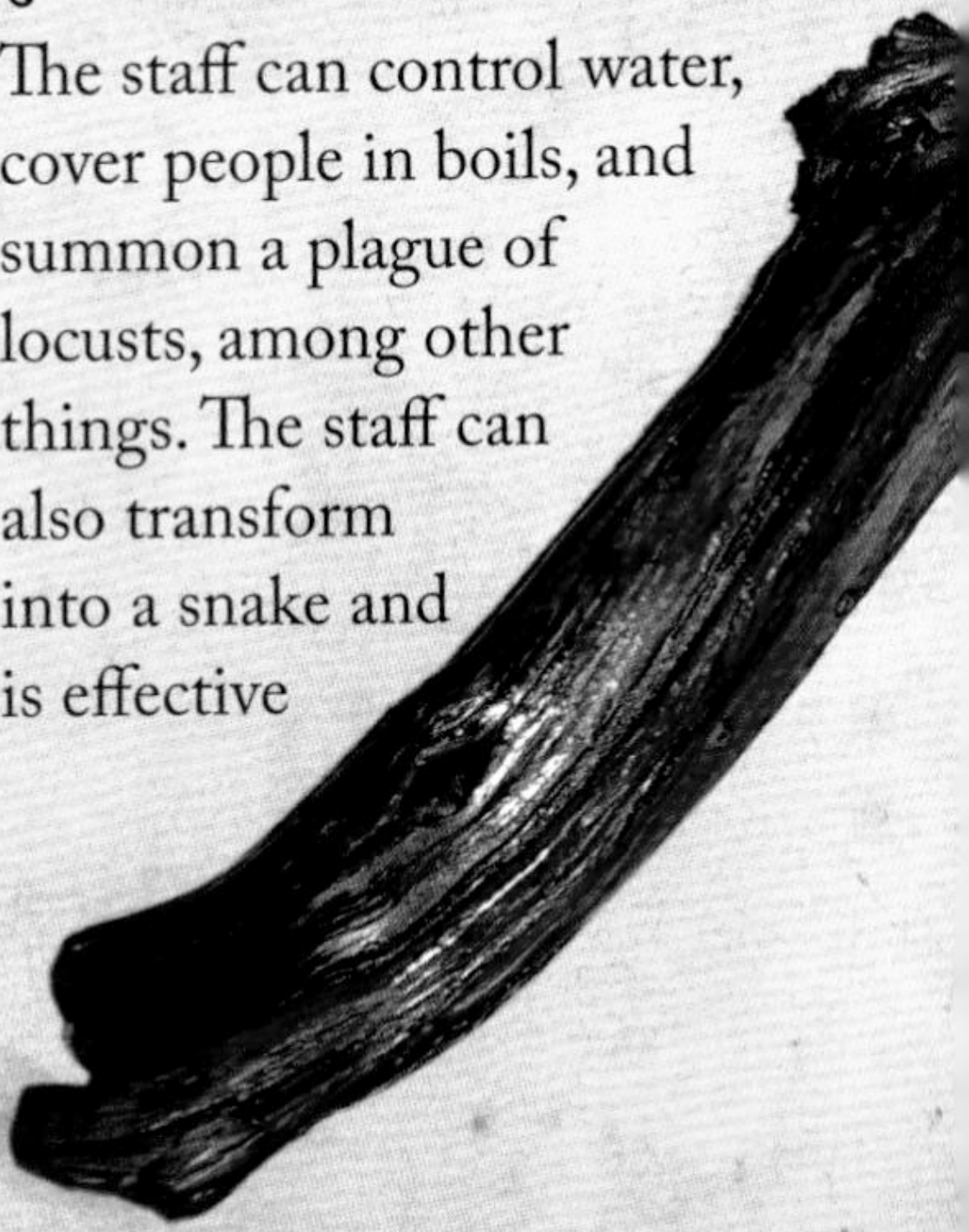

against angels in human vessels. Previously used by Moses in his display of dominance against the Egyptians, it is now in less potent pieces scattered throughout Heaven.

LOT'S SALT ROCK

Was used on humans when Lot's wife disobeyed the angels' order not to look back at Sodom, the doomed city her family was fleeing. Her eyes fell on the supercharged salt crystal, and she was instantly transformed into a pillar of salt.

GABRIEL'S HORN OF TRUTH

When blown, it compels all who hear it to speak the truth.

ARK OF THE COVENANT

Probably the most famous and most powerful of all heavenly weapons. Its true usage is unclear, but the Winchester's ally, the angel Castiel, doesn't refute that it's in the form of a gold box and that looking inside it will melt the faces off humans. It's the heavenly equivalent of a supernatural nuclear device.

HOLY FIRE

Holy Fire is a very effective weapon for fighting angels as it is Holy Oil set on fire. However, Holy Oil is a rare substance, and its composition and origins are unknown. A circle of Holy Fire will entrap an angel as surely as a Devil's Trap will hold a demon.

Holy Fire can also be used to burn angels out of their vessels or at least cause them to teleport to the nearest body of water.

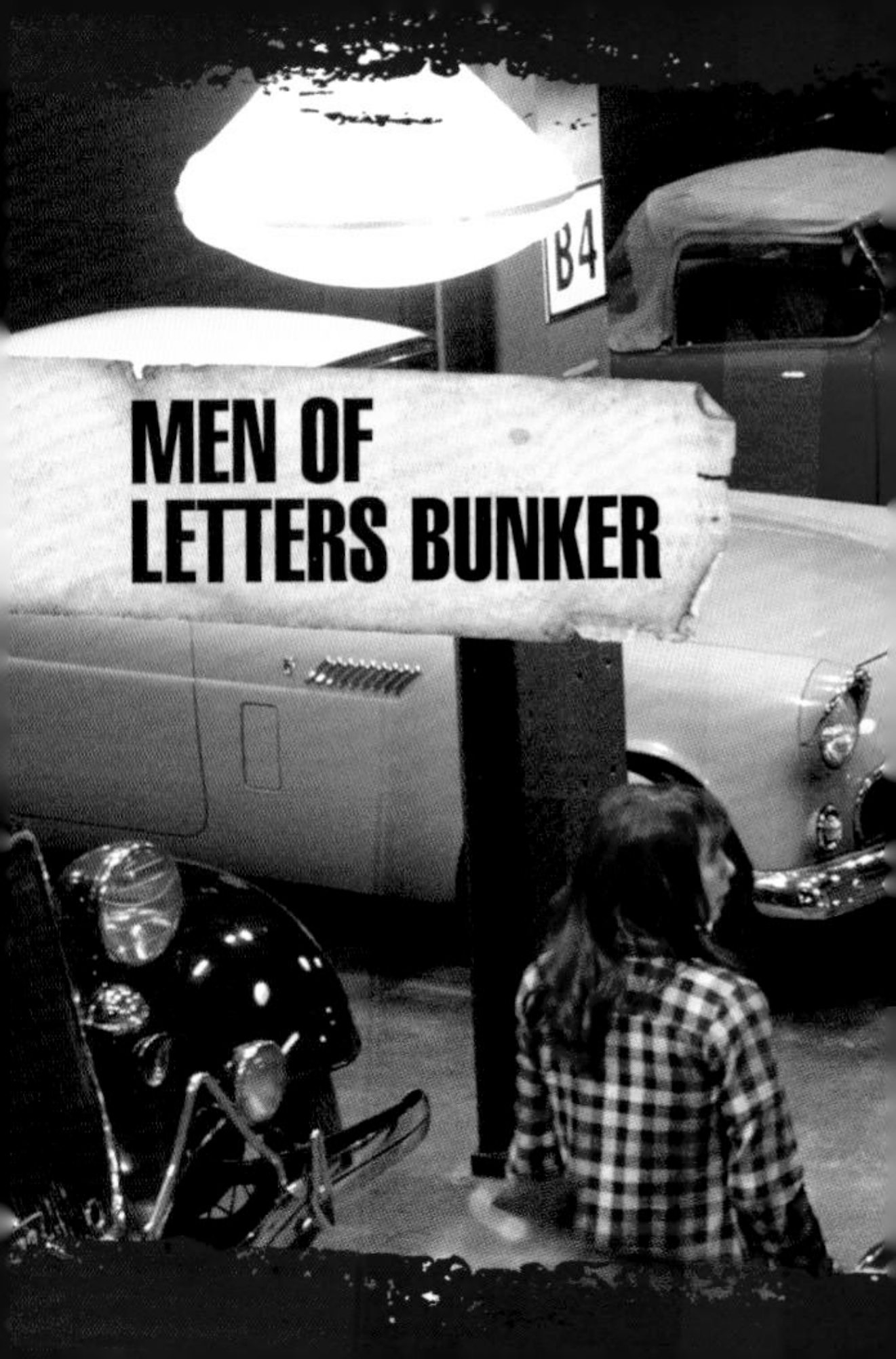
B4
MEN OF
LETTERS BUNKER

Upon Henry Winchester's death, Sam and Dean became Legacies and inherited the Men of Letters' sprawling underground bunker. The bunker is home to the Men of Letters' enormous library of research material, classified files, and enough weaponry and other items for combatting the supernatural to keep Sam and Dean stocked for the rest of their (un)natural lives.

In addition to a main meeting room with a large table covered by an illuminated world map, the bunker contains a fully stocked research library, an observatory, a crow's nest, a laboratory,

a kitchen, multiple bedrooms, a dungeon, and one hell of a garage, complete with vintage automobiles from the 1950s.

THINGS THAT GO BUMP IN THE NIGHT

There are too many monsters lurking around every corner to count, much less describe in detail, but what follows is a primer on some of the supernatural beings Dean and Sam have encountered in past years.

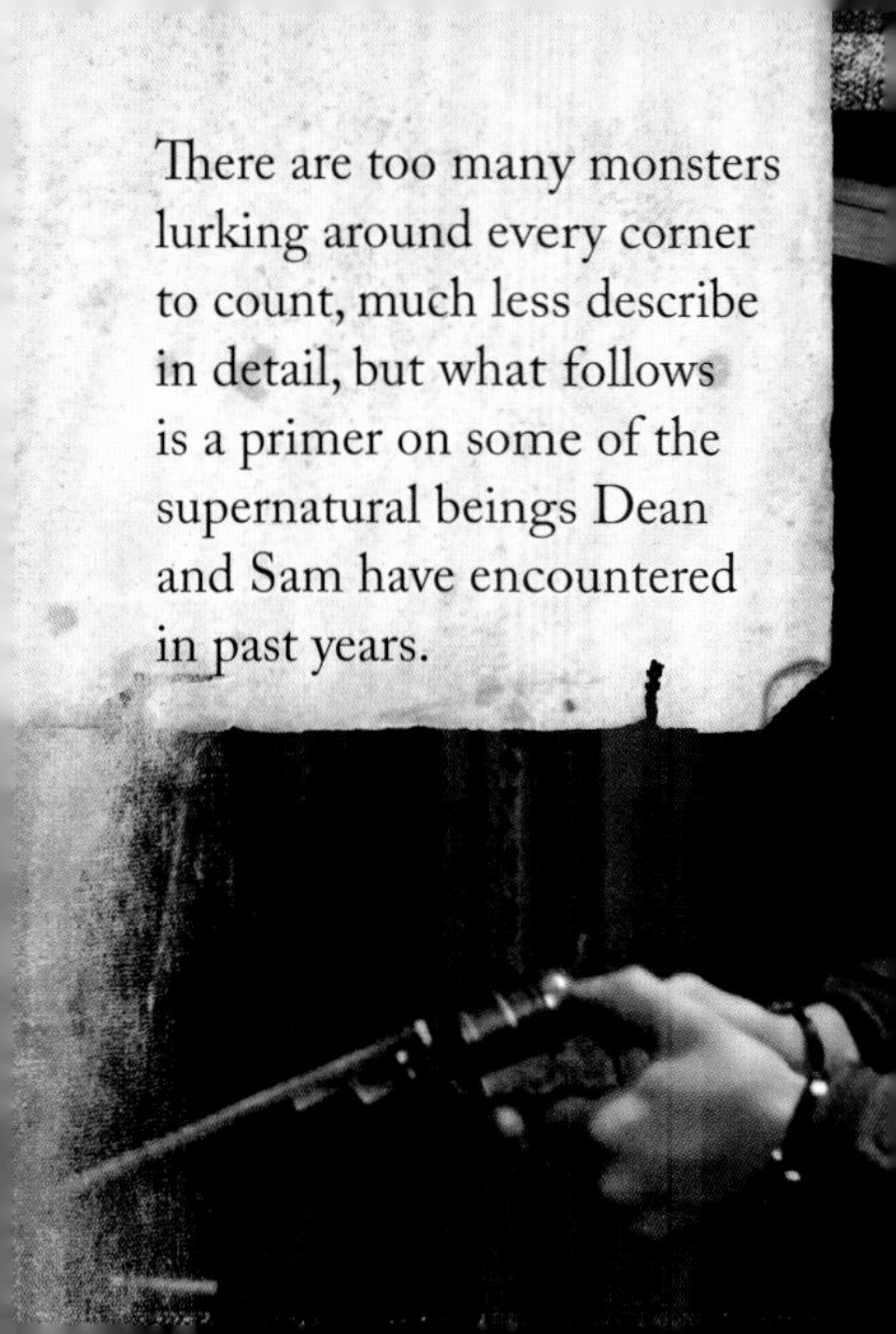

ANTICHRIST

Born of a demon-possessed virgin human, the Antichrist is possessed of almost limitless supernatural abilities and can destroy the "Host of Heaven" with a single word. The Antichrist's powers include telekinesis, teleportation, exorcising demons with his mind, and making even the simplest of thoughts a reality. The Antichrist is impossible to kill but can be persuaded to never use his powers again if reasoned with compassionately.

CHANGELINGS

A supernatural creature that mimics the appearance and behavior of human children in order to feed off of their human mothers, and will kill anyone who tries to stop them. The changeling mother will feed the human children who have been abducted and replaced. Changelings can be destroyed by fire, and when the changeling mother is killed, her brood dies with her.

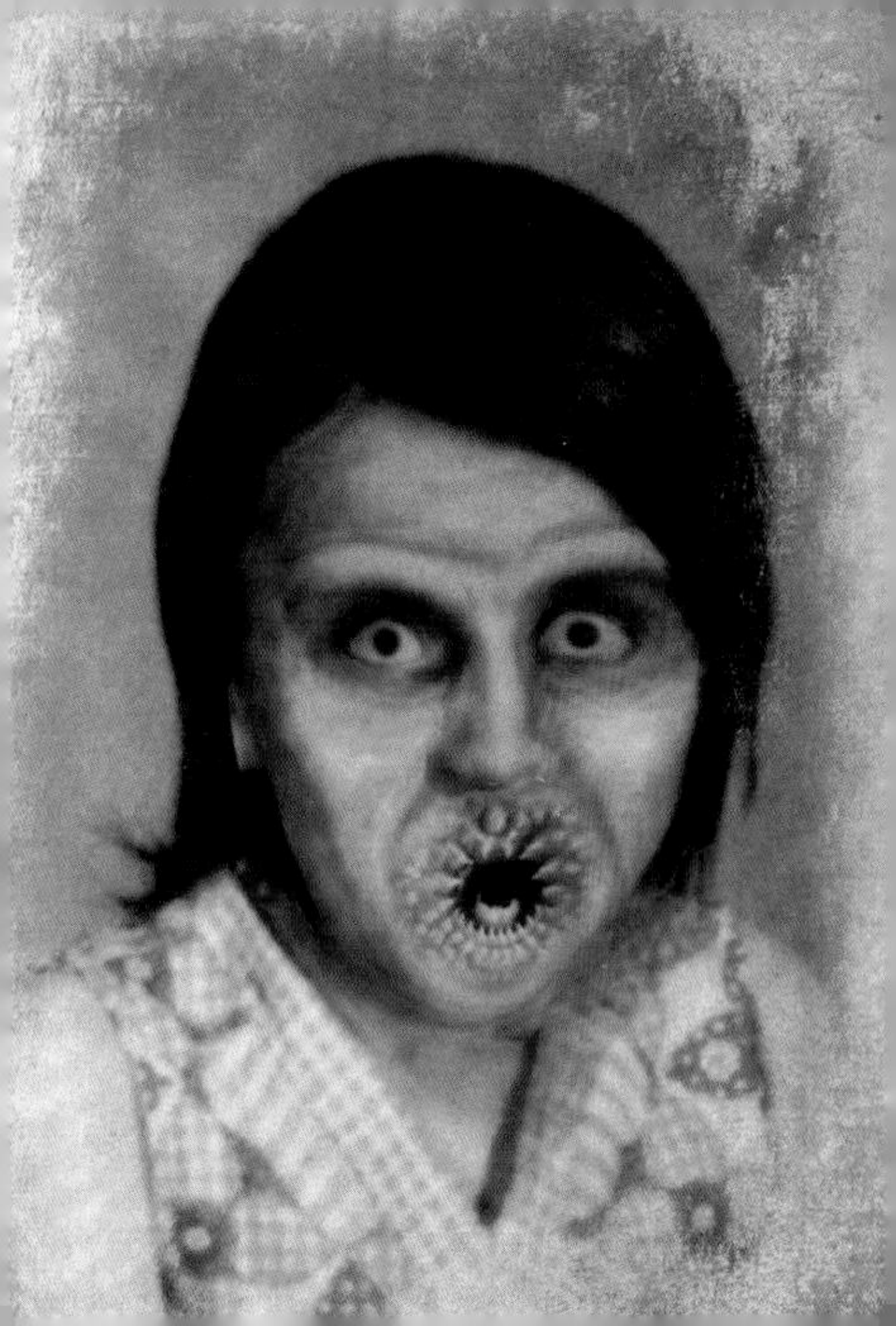

DJINN (GENIES)

Essentially evil genies, djinn are creatures of smokeless fire, but their solid human form is indistinguishable from regular humans. With just a touch, they make their victim's greatest wish come true—but only inside their victims' minds. These supernatural hallucinations feel so real that the victims rarely try to wake up. Meanwhile, the djinn will feed on

the victim's bodily fluids. Djinn can be killed with a silver knife dipped in lamb's blood.

GHOSTS

Spirits of the deceased that are trapped on Earth. They can walk through walls, the stronger ones can move objects and kill people, and they'll haunt just about anything—loved ones, houses, hotels, mental asylums, cars, boats, roads, flasks—and some ghosts can even infect people like a disease, making them so afraid of everything that their hearts burst.

They're usually tethered to their bones, so if they've been cremated, look for other remains of theirs that would have some DNA attached, like a friendship bracelet with blood on it or a wig made out of their hair or even a donated kidney.

GHOULS

Ghouls are monster scavengers that eat the dead and take on the likenesses, thoughts, and memories of their victims' last meal. Usually they dig up graves and eat the corpses, but they may also come after the living. They can only be killed by decapitation or the destruction of their heads.

KHAN WORM

A creation of Eve, the Mother of All Monsters, the Khan worm is a parasitic worm that crawls into humans' ears and takes control of their bodies. It turns friends and family against each other with deadly consequences, and was a tool developed by Eve as a means of exterminating humankind. It can be killed with electric current.

PAGAN GODS

Pagan gods are supernatural entities that gain their power from humans worshipping them as gods. They like to eat humans, but they're not greedy; they provide their worshippers with bountiful harvests, good health, and protection from other hungry pagan gods in return for a relatively small number of human sacrifices.

REAPERS

Reapers are spirit-like creatures that usually appear in human form. They reap souls for Death, can stop time and alter human perception, and will use any methods they can think of to get the newly dead to cross over to the afterlife. The living can't see them, so you have to use astral projection, kill yourself to find them, or use an angel or demon as your go-between, as they can see reapers easily.

SHAPESHIFTERS AND SKINWALKERS

These monsters have the ability to transform into exact replicas of humans or animals. They study your routines and mannerisms, then take on your appearance and steal your memories to mimic you perfectly. Some can change their appearance, while others must shed their old skins when their new form emerges. All shapeshifters and skinwalkers can be killed with a silver bullet or other sharp silver object to the heart.

SHTRIGAS

A ghastly-looking soul-sucker; shtrigas are a type of witch that feeds by sucking the "breath of life" out of people. They prefer children because their life forces are strongest, but any human will do. They target sick, suicidal, or otherwise weak people because their life forces are not attached as strongly to their bodies. They can only be killed by consecrated wrought iron.

SIRENS

Sirens have pale skin, hollow eyes, and a scary mouth, but they usually take on human forms. They can read minds and use what they learn to take on the guise of someone their intended victims will desire being with, then they use their toxic saliva to turn their victims into adoring slaves. The only way to kill a siren is with a bronze dagger dipped in the blood of someone it has infected.

VAMPIRES

Vampires are "turned" humans who have extra-sharp, retractable teeth and crave human blood. They nest in packs and sleep in cocoon-style hammocks; they need to feed on mammalian blood to survive, and human blood tastes the best.

They sire new vampires by force-feeding people their infected blood. Crosses do not repel them, and direct sunlight will burn them but not kill them—and nor will a stake through the heart. Vampires can only be killed through beheading.

WENDIGO

A wendigo is an individual who has eaten human flesh in conjunction with black magic and gained inhuman speed and strength, as well as immortality. They're bigger than humans, their teeth and nails are monstrously long, and their eyes glow. To catch their prey, they lure hikers deep into the forest and then hold them prisoner in their underground lairs until feeding time. They can only be killed with fire.

WEREWOLVES

A person infected by lycanthropy will turn into a ravenous, supernaturally strong human-wolf hybrid known as a werewolf during the full moon. Although they act like feral animals, werewolves tend to hunt and kill people who have angered them in their human lives. If it wasn't for this connection, they might never find out they're werewolves, as they don't seem to retain any memories of their monstrous behavior.

Whatever you do, don't get bitten. Don't listen to hunters who tell you that killing the werewolf that bit you will lift the curse, as there is no cure. Werewolves can only be killed by a silver bullet.

WITCHES

Witches are humans who use dark magic to perform curses, summon demons, and even swap bodies. They need to use various combinations of spells, sigils, effigies, hex bags, and animal sacrifices to affect others magically. Usually, they use magic to enrich their own lives and torture their enemies. Witches can be killed using conventional weapons.

WRAITHS

A humanoid creature that gets close to other humans in order to eat their brains. A wraith has a spike that pops out of its wrist when it's feeding. Wraiths enjoy the taste of "insane" brains and are usually found near mental institutions. They are capable of causing hallucinations and other emotional changes through physical touch.

Wraiths will die if they go too long without feeding on human flesh and can also be killed with a weapon made of pure silver.

ZOMBIES

A dead person reanimated by Death or through necromancy. They often try to go back to their old lives but are driven by a hunger for revenge and will happily kill anyone who wronged them in life. They seem normal at first, but eventually their hunger for human flesh will escalate, turning them into a stereotypical zombie. They can be killed by staking, beheading, or otherwise destroying their heads.

"We know a little about a lot of things; just enough to make us dangerous."

—DEAN WINCHESTER

THE HIERARCHY OF DEMONS

Demons are human souls that were sent to Hell and became twisted into evil spirits. God preferred humans to angels and Lucifer became jealous. To provoke God, he tempted a human soul and twisted it into the very first demon. This action is what got him locked up in his supernatural cage downstairs.

Demons mostly reside in Hell, but when demons can escape to our world, they rarely stay incorporeal, preferring instead to possess humans, which they refer to as meat-suits. They have superhuman strength and telekinetic abilities, and they love to torture people.

Exorcisms expel demons from people's bodies, which is useful because it keeps the body intact, but doing so just sends the demon back to Hell. It's best to destroy them with a demon-killing knife or shoot them with the Colt, though that will kill their meat-suit as well.

When hunting demons, the best way to spot them is to look for traces of sulfur, lightning storms, and cattle mutilations, which they tend to leave behind wherever they've been. They can't cross lines of salt, iron and holy water burns them, Palo Santo (Holy Wood) can pin them down, and a Devil's Trap works as advertised. Additionally, saying any of God's names will make them flinch and flash their demon eyes.

WHITE-EYED DEMONS

These demons are the chiefs of staff.

LILITH

Lilith was the first demon ever created. In keeping with her white eyes, her signature attack is a devastating blast of white energy. Because she is the Queen of the Crossroads, all Crossroads Demons make deals for her, which is why she ultimately holds sway over Dean Winchester's soul and plots to use Dean to break the first seal binding Lucifer to his cage.

Lilith loves Lucifer and willingly sacrifices herself, allowing Sam to kill her, knowing that as the first demon, she is the last seal binding Lucifer to his cage.

ALASTAIR

Alastair is very old and powerful, possibly the second demon ever created. He is Hell's master torturer, and he tortured both John and Dean Winchester when they were in Hell. When Castiel and Alastair battle each other, Alastair gets the upper hand on Castiel and nearly sends him back to Heaven with an Enochian spell, but Sam arrives and uses his psychic demon powers to first torture and then kill Alastair.

RED-EYED DEMONS

These are the Crossroad Demons, demon dealmakers who make deals for the souls that fuel Hell. They can grant humans practically any wish, making their powers on par with reality-altering angels like Zachariah. It's unknown how many Crossroad Demons there are, but Crowley is the most powerful.

CROWLEY

Crowley is Lilith's right-hand man and King of the Crossroads. As a human he was a Scottish tailor named Fergus Roderick McLeod who sold his soul for three additional inches below the waist. His wish-granting capabilities seem to have no limits. After Lilith and Alastair are killed and Lucifer is locked up again, Crowley crowns himself the King of Hell.

He's nasty, cocky, brutally honest, and wickedly funny. If he weren't such a bad guy, he'd make one amazing hero—although technically he is a hero to the forces of evil.

YELLOW-EYED DEMONS

These are the demon army generals.

AZAZEL

Azazel is the only known Yellow-Eyed Demon and is the catalyst for everything that Sam and Dean Winchester have gone through. He killed their grandparents and their father, John, whom he then resurrected in return for future access to baby Sam. When he kills Mary Winchester, Sam and Dean are pushed farther into becoming hunters.

- Acheri are demons that disguise themselves as little girls, albeit with superlong fingernails coated in blood.
- The Seven Deadly Sins thrive on causing the sin they represent.
- Samhain, the Lord of the Dead, raises ghosts, ghouls, zombies, and other beasts on All Hallows' Eve.
- Croatoan are virus-sized demons that fill people with demonic rage and are passed by blood-to-blood contact.

RUBY

Ruby is Lilith's most loyal follower. She initially appears to be just another hunter—one who happens to have a knife that kills demons. But even when the Winchesters learn she's a demon, she makes them wonder whether she could actually be a good one.

Ultimately, Ruby helps Sam to kill Lilith, which appears to be a good thing until the Winchesters find out that Ruby has kept an important fact from them: Killing Lilith breaks the final seal that frees Lucifer from Hell. Ruby's victorious gloating is short-lived, as Sam grabs hold of her and Dean stabs her with her own demon-killing knife.

MEG

Meg is Azazel's "daughter" and enters the Winchesters' lives as a potential love interest for Sam, but it isn't long before she reveals that she's a demon. The brothers manage to exorcise her multiple times, but she keeps returning in different bodies.

When Crowley becomes King of Hell, Meg attempts to use Castiel as a weapon against Crowley, but her plan backfires, and she is captured and taken back to Hell.

THE KNIGHTS OF HELL

CAIN

Centuries ago, Lucifer tried to corrupt Cain's younger brother, Abel, and make the young man his special "pet." In order to prevent this, Cain made a deal with Lucifer that Abel's soul would be kept safe in Heaven in exchange for his own soul, which Lucifer would keep in Hell.

Lucifer agreed, but only on the condition that Cain kill Abel himself. Cain murdered his brother with a donkey's jawbone, which then became known as the First Blade. Lucifer marked Cain with a special brand that gave the First Blade its power and made Cain a demon—the first of Lucifer's Knights of Hell. Cain then led his fellow Knights as they wreaked havoc across the Earth.

ABBADON

Abaddon is a demon Knight of Hell and the last of her kind. She returned to Earth to claim control of Hell from Crowley and turn all of humankind into her demon army. She was killed by Dean when he used the First Blade on her.

A GUIDE TO ANGELS

Angels are warriors of God. They are colossal, winged beings that are multidimensional wavelengths of celestial intent. Their true forms will burn human eyes out, and their true voices will shatter glass and burst human eardrums, so they communicate via electronics (like TVs and radios) when necessary. However, they will usually take on a human host.

Angels can see demons' true faces and are only too happy to smite them immediately. Devoid of free will and human emotions, they'll follow their orders blindly, even if that means killing other angels, eradicating thousands of humans, or actually helping fallen archangel Lucifer start the Apocalypse.

Angels can teleport at will, knock a human out cold with a touch, and enter a person's dreams. They can even travel through time, but the act takes an enormous physical toll on them.

Although awe-inspiring, they do have some weaknesses: A circle of Holy Fire will trap them, and both Holy Fire and heavenly weapons can destroy their human vessels. Plus, there are three things that can kill them: a Leviathan, one of their own angel blades, and the archangels.

There are only four archangels—Michael, Lucifer, Raphael, and Gabriel—and they are God's most terrifying warriors, able to obliterate a "regular" angel with a simple snap of their fingers.

ENOCHIAN

Enochian is the language of angels, which they use to communicate with one another in Heaven and on Earth. It is also used in spells that involve angels, whether one is summoning, binding, or expelling them. There is an Enochian chant that can forcibly expel an angel from its human vessel and send it back to Heaven.

Enochian sigils are glyphs of immense power used to bind demons, protect individuals from angelic detection, and prevent angels from entering or discovering spaces such as houses, rooms, or great swaths of land.

ANGELS FROM A TO Z

ANNA

Anna was Castiel's superior in Heaven, but she ripped out her Grace and fell to Earth so that she could experience love and chocolate. When the first seal on Lucifer's cage is broken, the now-human Anna starts hearing angels broadcasting messages. She wants to remain human, but with demons trying to use her to spy on the angels and angels trying to kill her for removing her Grace, she has no choice but to reinsert it.

She goes on the run but eventually returns to save Castiel from the rogue angel Uriel. Castiel, ever the good soldier, still sends Anna to prison in Heaven, but she eventually escapes and travels back in time to try to kill John and Mary Winchester before they can give birth to Sam, Lucifer's vessel. Ironically, Anna gets a younger Uriel to help her, but then the Archangel Michael possesses John and smites her.

BALTHAZAR

Balthazar once fought alongside Castiel, but he now believes it's a new era with no rules and no destiny—just utter and complete freedom. He fakes his own death to live on Earth and remains an ally of sorts, assisting Castiel a few times.

When he discovers Castiel is working with the demon Crowley, he spies on his friend for the Winchesters and pays for his betrayal when he's literally stabbed in the back by Castiel.

BARTHOLOMEW

The angel Bartholomew was perhaps the biggest thorn in Castiel's side. After falling to Earth, Bartholomew consolidated his power by finding human vessels to contain thousands of displaced angels, thus creating an unstoppable army.

Castiel refused to ally with Bartholomew and was able to overpower and kill him. Realizing Castiel represented the best way forward, many of Bartholomew's followers declared their allegiance to the rebel angel.

CASTIEL

Angel. Soldier of God. Defender of humans. Castiel is all these things and more, and from his very first appearance, he has established himself as one of the most powerful and intriguing figures to enter the Winchesters' lives. His powers are vast, proven from the beginning, when he pulled Dean out of the very depths of Hell to once again walk the Earth and fulfill his mission to stop the impending Apocalypse.

He can also travel to the past, become invisible to humans, incinerate monsters, and smite demons with a simple touch. In the Winchesters' fight against evil, Castiel is an invaluable ally. But he is not without his flaws. His bond with Dean and his affection for humans makes him weak in the eyes of other angels.

Castiel touchingly proves himself a little bit human along the way, until he declares himself the new God and destroys anyone—and anything—that stands in his way. Later, he absorbs the evil creatures known as Leviathan; unable to contain them, he implodes, freeing them to roam the planet.

Castiel returns, months later, a changed angel who cannot remember his past. Eventually, while working with the Winchesters, he remembers who he is and embarks on a quest to right his wrongs.

"Now I realize that there is no righteous path, it's just people trying to do their best in a world where it is far too easy to do your worst."

—CASTIEL

GABRIEL

Gabriel is the archangel formerly known as the Trickster. He disguised himself as the pagan god Loki in order to hide from his squabbling brothers, Michael and Lucifer, but he nonetheless takes a special interest in the human brothers destined to become Michael and Lucifer's vessels, Dean and Sam Winchester.

His relationship with the Winchesters eventually causes him to take the side of the humans and battle Lucifer, dying valiantly.

GADREEL

The angel Gadreel was one of God's most trusted angels and was tasked with protecting Paradise. When he failed in this task, he was imprisoned in one of Heaven's darkest dungeons for thousands of years. When Metatron's spell expelled all the angels from Heaven, Gadreel was freed.

Gadreel pretended to be the much-respected angel Ezekiel and promised to help the Winchester brothers, but he ultimately joined Metatron's cause before realizing

he was just a disposable pawn in Metatron's plan to become the new God. He finally found redemption by sacrificing himself so that Castiel could put a stop to Metatron's master plan.

HESTER

A member of Castiel's former angel garrison in Heaven. Believing Castiel to be dead, she arrives on Earth to protect the new Prophet of the Lord, Kevin Tran, from harm. Hester is shocked to learn that Castiel is alive, but she is eventually killed by Meg when she tries to kill Castiel.

JOSHUA

Joshua is Heaven's gardener. Even as most angels are starting to feel like God has left the building, Joshua claims to have conversations with God, though they're mostly one-way. When the brothers are trapped in Heaven, he saves Sam and Dean from Zachariah in order to deliver a message to them from God Himself.

METATRON

Metatron was an angel scribe who recorded the Word of God on two tablets that have since become weapons in the war between angels and the demons. When the archangels realized they needed both Metatron and the two tablets to take over the universe themselves, Metatron fled to Earth, where he sequestered himself in a Colorado motel and plotted his revenge.

MICHAEL

As the oldest and most powerful archangel, Michael wants Lucifer to rise from Hell so that they can have an apocalyptic grudge match. But Castiel interrupts his plans when he destroys Michael's planned human vessel (Adam Milligan) with Holy Fire, and then Sam Winchester yanks Michael down into Lucifer's cage in Hell, where the two angels wrestle on in a never-ending battle.

NAOMI

A powerful agent from Heaven's intelligence division, Naomi was ruthless in her quest to prevent the angel tablet from falling into the wrong hands. She was the one who brought Castiel back from Purgatory and used him as her spy on Earth until he rebelled and severed his connection to her. She was killed by Metatron.

RAPHAEL

Raphael is a staunch supporter of his archangel brother Michael. After the first seal is broken, he does everything he can to bring on the Apocalypse so that Michael and Lucifer can end their eons-old spat once and for all. He won't let anything stop him—not even Castiel, whom he kills and then continues to war with in his resurrected form.

When Castiel takes on God-like powers of his own thanks to the souls from Purgatory, Raphael is simply wiped out of existence by a snap of the now-powerful angel's fingers.

URIEL

An angel purification specialist who feels that dealing with humans is a waste of his time. He claims he can turn humans to dust just by uttering one word, but he is kept in line by Castiel. Uriel secretly plots to break seals and kills any angels that refuse to help him free Lucifer. Once he fails to convert Castiel to his cause, he plans to make him his next victim, but Anna kills Uriel first.

VIRGIL

Virgil is an angel assassin that Raphael sends to retrieve the heavenly weapons from Balthazar, but the crafty rogue angel whips up a spell that sends Virgil chasing after the Winchester brothers to an alternate universe, where he remains trapped to this day.

ZACHARIAH

As part of Heaven's upper management, Zachariah was consistently employee of the month in Heaven before his failure to recruit Sam and Dean Winchester as vessels for Lucifer and Michael made him a laughingstock. Zachariah thinks his luck's finally changed when Dean agrees to become Michael's vessel, only to discover it was a ruse for Dean to get close enough to kill him with an angel blade.

THE 66 SEALS

What are they? Locks on the door of Lucifer's Cage.

How many are there? 600

How do they work? Break 66 and Lucifer is freed from Hell.

Is there a combination? The first and last are crucial, but the middle 64 can be any of the other 598.

The first seal: The first seal is broken when a righteous man—in this case Dean Winchester—sheds blood in Hell.

The final seal: Lilith dies. As it is written, "The first demon will be the last seal."

LUCIFER: KING OF HELL

Lucifer. Satan. The Devil. Beelzebub. Serpent King. Lord of the Flies. Prince of Darkness. Father of Lies. Ruler of Hell. Call him what you will—just don't call him a demon, as he is actually a fallen archangel.

He did, however, create demons, and for that God imprisoned him in Hell. Lucifer truly believes that he was wronged by God for not bowing down to humans, who he sees as flawed, violent, fragile little creatures. When Sam Winchester frees him from his cage, Lucifer wants revenge on humans, on his archangel brothers, and on God himself.

After he convinces Sam to become his new vessel, Lucifer

reveals his greatest weakness: vanity. He overestimates his suppression of Sam's will and underestimates the power of familial love, losing control of Sam's body just long enough for Sam to drag him back to Hell.

"Why not just serve your own best interests? Which in this case just happen to be mine?"

—LUCIFER

THE FOUR HORSEMEN

The Four Horsemen—War, Famine, Pestilence, and Death—are destructive forces of nature. When they show themselves to humans, they do so with great dramatic flare. War has been seen riding a red horse and driving a red Ford Mustang; Famine a black horse and a black Cadillac Escalade; Pestilence a pale green

horse and a sickly green AMC Hornet; and Death a white horse and a white Cadillac Eldorado.

All of the Horsemen can teleport, and they each have special supernatural talents:

War reads minds and gives people hallucinations that make them fight with one another.

Famine consumes souls (human or demon) and makes people so hungry for the things they crave the most that they're willing to kill for them.

Pestilence creates horrific and incurable diseases; and Death commands reapers and raises the dead.

Lucifer gathers them to him in preparation of the Apocalypse. War, Famine, and Pestilence don't seem to mind following Lucifer's orders, but Death—who is far more powerful than the other Horsemen—does not like being bound to Lucifer. He willingly gives Dean his ring, as the combined rings are the key to sending Lucifer back to his cage in Hell.

LEVIATHAN

Long before God created angels and humans, he made the first beasts: the Leviathan. Clever and nearly invulnerable, they had a bad habit of eating everything God subsequently created. They even killed angels, leading God to create a Purgatory in which to lock the Leviathan away—until Castiel inadvertently let them back into the world.

In their natural state, they appear as a black goo that can travel through fluids, but once they possess a human body, they are able to shapeshift into any other human they touch. Their large, sharp tooth–filled mouths can expand to engulf a person's head. They have superstrength and regenerate quickly from wounds.

Leviathan can actually stop other Leviathan. There is a hierarchy to their society, in which underlings are often eaten if they displease their superiors. A particularly cruel punishment, known as bibbing, involves Leviathan being forced to eat themselves. But there's little chance of the Leviathan eating one another into extinction—not when there are billions of humans ripe for the picking.

ADDITIONAL HUNTERS AND ALLIES

BOBBY SINGER

There is one person hunters turn to when they need help or want to network with other hunters: Bobby Singer. Bobby is a surrogate father to Sam and Dean Winchester. When he's not hunting, researching supernatural threats, answering the phone in the guise of a variety of fake federal agents, or building monster-proof panic rooms, he runs an auto salvage yard.

Bobby became a hunter after he had to kill his demon-possessed wife, Karen. He was shown the ropes by Rufus Turner, whom he hunted with until "the incident" in Omaha. Even when he stays home, he can't avoid hunting, occasionally getting attacked by ghosts and zombies.

With everything he's been through, Bobby no doubt expected to be eaten by a monster someday, but he loses his life to a regular bullet. Yet, even in death Bobby is not willing to lose everything. He hangs on to his life as a ghost haunting his old flask. However, the risk of becoming a vengeful spirit is too great and he insists Sam and Dean burn the flask, and Bobby leaves the Winchesters' lives forever.

"Hell, I'm already dead, what's the worst that could happen?"

—BOBBY SINGER

ELLEN HARVELLE

Aside from networking through Bobby, hunters have been known to exchange horror stories over brews at Harvelle's Roadhouse. Ellen Harvelle is the owner and operator. Her husband, Bill, died while on a hunt with John Winchester, and she has tried to keep her daughter, Jo, from becoming a hunter.

However, it's a matter of "Do as I say, not as I do," because Ellen is a top-notch hunter in her own right and helps Bobby close the Devil's Gate. Years later, she sacrifices her life to help Sam and Dean (try to) kill Lucifer.

JO HARVELLE

Jo Harvelle rebels against her mother, running away from the Roadhouse to follow in her father's hunting footsteps. She's handy with knives and shotguns but inexperienced with actual hunting, and she almost dies on her first case at the hands of a serial killer ghost before the Winchesters save her.

Over time she becomes a truly kickass hunter, even teaming up with her mother on occasion. In the battle against Lucifer, Jo is mortally wounded by Meg's Hellhound and dies in her mother's arms.

ASH

Harvelle's Roadhouse welcomes a regular flow of hunters through its doors, but one customer—Ash—likes it there so much that he sleeps in a back room or on the pool table. Even though he got kicked out of MIT for fighting, he's a hacker, not a fighter, so he does his hunting through his computer. He even created specialized demon-tracking software.

Ash's love of the Roadhouse is his downfall, as he dies inside it when it's burned down. But he carries on in Heaven, where his personal version of the afterlife looks like Harvelle's, and his computer now tracks angels instead of demons.

RUFUS TURNER

Due to whatever unspeakable thing happened in the past with Bobby in Omaha, Rufus Turner is a somewhat reluctant ally. The two still turn to each other for help with tasks, but their friendship unexpectedly ends when Bobby becomes possessed by a monster and kills Rufus.

GARTH

Another very different hunter acquaintance of Bobby's is Garth. Monsters don't get ganked by Garth; they get "Garthed." He usually hunts alone, but he has his sock puppet, Mr. Fizzles, to keep him company. At the end of a hunt, Garth doesn't relax at a place like Harvelle's—he's literally a one-drink drunk—he'd much rather ease his weary bones in a hot tub. When he does hunt with friends, he never lets them part ways without a good hug.

JODY MILLS

Sheriff Jody Mills didn't start out wanting to be a hunter. Even after seeing her undead son eat her husband and having to shoot said son in the head, Jody doesn't actively pursue hunting. She does, however, change her opinion of Bobby, whom she used to think was nothing more than a crazy drunk.

In fact, sparks fly between Jody and Bobby. Bobby's death comes as a shock to her, but it motivates her to use her police connections

to watch out for supernatural-related cases on behalf of Dean and Sam.

FRANK DEVEREAUX

Frank Devereaux is not exactly a hunter. He's not exactly sane, either, but he is a very useful ally. When the Leviathan learn all of Sam and Dean's aliases, Frank provides them with new identities and coaches them on ways to keep a lower profile; he even teaches Dean how to hack into security camera feeds.

Frank's continued research into Leviathan leader Dick Roman's activities makes him a target, and the last Sam and Dean see of him is a mobile trailer full of blood.

GORDON WALKER

Gordon Walker became a hunter obsessed with killing vampires when his sister was turned into a bloodsucker. He thinks all vampires are evil without exception. However, Gordon comes to believe that Sam is the Antichrist and becomes so focused on killing him that even being turned into a vampire himself doesn't distract him from what he believes to be his righteous mission.

BELA TALBOT

Bela Talbot is a master thief with a special knack for communicating with ghosts. She specializes in stealing and selling supernatural objects. When she steals a cursed rabbit's foot from John Winchester's storage unit, she runs afoul of Sam and Dean.

Bela later steals the Colt from the brothers. She had made a deal with a Crossroads Demon when she was younger in exchange for having her abusive parents killed. When her contract comes due, she

tries to trade the Colt for her soul, giving it to Lilith's right-hand man, Crowley. But he keeps the Colt instead, and Bela goes to Hell.

BENNY LAFITTE

Benny was a vampire trapped in Purgatory who became a friend and ally of Dean Winchester during his time there. Despite Dean's mistrust of vampires, Benny quickly proved himself a worthy ally, and the two worked together to both protect each other and formulate a plan to escape.

Once back on Earth, Dean and Benny remained in regular communication and helped each other out when needed. Benny's

relationship with Dean was one of the closest the elder Winchester brother had had with a non-family member for some time, but Benny meets his demise helping Sam escape.

KEVIN TRAN

Kevin is the latest Prophet of the Lord thanks to his contact with the angel tablet, the object previously sought by former Leviathan leader Dick Roman. He can translate the angel and demon tablets. He finds himself working with the Winchester brothers despite his reluctance at being drawn into their never-ending battle with the forces of evil.

CHARLIE BRADBURY

One of the Winchester brothers' most unique and talented allies, Charlie continues to aid Sam and Dean when she can with her computer skills. The brothers are always happy to see Charlie, as the cases she is involved in tend to be welcome breaks from the larger struggles that they face. She is like the little sister they never had.

AMELIA RICHARDSON

Amelia was a veterinarian who worked at the River Bluff Veterinary Hospital. Sam and Amelia struck up a friendship that blossomed into something deeper. They eventually shared a house together for almost a year before Amelia discovered that her husband, who she believed died in Afghanistan, was in fact alive. This revelation led Sam to leave Texas so that Amelia could have a chance to reconnect with her husband.

THE CAMPBELLS: HUNTERS OF OLD

The Campbell family, including Mary and her parents, Deanna and Samuel Campbell, were all hunters long before John Winchester became one. The Campbells are a family line of hunters going back further than the first settlers of the United States, some of whom were

hacking the heads off of vampires on the *Mayflower.*

Despite their hunting pedigree, they are not immune to demonic dangers. The Campbell family has found themselves on the losing side of some battles, leaving Sam and Dean the only members left to honor their family's hunting legacy:

- Deanna (grandmother): Killed by Azazel.
- Samuel (grandfather): Possessed and killed by Azazel. Resurrected by Crowley and makes a deal with the Crossroads Demon, but Sam kills him when he is infected by the Khan worm.
- Mary (mother): Mary makes a deal with Azazel, trading John Winchester's life for access to

baby Sam, only to be murdered herself by Azazel years later.

- Christian (cousin): Gets possessed by a demon and spies on his hunting kin, then killed by the Alpha Vampire.
- Gwen (cousin): Killed by Dean, who was infected by the Khan worm.
- Johnny: Killed by a djinn.
- Mark: Killed by the Alpha Shapeshifter.
- Ed and Robert: Killed by Azazel to keep John Winchester off the demon's trail.

"We're the guys that
save the world."

—SAM WINCHESTER

"This book. This is Dad's single most valuable possession. Everything he knows about every evil thing is in here. And he's passed it on to us. I think he wants us to pick up where he left off. You know, saving people, hunting things. The family business."

—DEAN WINCHESTER

INSIGHT
EDITIONS

PO Box 3088
San Rafael, CA 94912
www.insighteditions.com

Find us on Facebook:
www.facebook.com/InsightEditions
Follow us on Twitter: @insighteditions

Copyright © 2023 Warner Bros. Entertainment
SUPERNATURAL and all related characters and elements
© & ™ WBEI. WB SHIELD: ™ & © Warner Bros.
Entertainment Inc. (s23)

INED41233

All rights reserved. Published by Insight Editions, San Rafael, California, in 2018. No part of this book may be reproduced in any form without written permission from the publisher.

978-1-68383-589-9

Manufactured in China by Insight Editions

10 9 8 7 6 5 4 3 2